P9-AFE-540

CINDERELLA

A FAVORITE STORY IN RHYTHM AND RHYME

Retold by SUSAN SANDVIG WALKER
Illustrated by LUCY FLEMING
Music Arranged and Produced by DREW TEMPERANTE

CANTATA
LEARNING

WWW.CANTATALEARNING.COM

CANTATA LEARNING

Published by Cantata Learning
1710 Roe Crest Drive
North Mankato, MN 56003
www.cantatalearning.com

A note to educators and librarians from the publisher: Cantata Learning has provided the following data to assist in book processing and suggested use of Cantata Learning product.

Publisher's Cataloging-in-Publication Data
Prepared by Librarian Consultant: Ann-Marie Begnaud
Library of Congress Control Number: 2015958176
    Cinderella : A Favorite Story in Rhythm and Rhyme
    Series: Fairy Tale Tunes
    Retold by Susan Sandvig Walker
    Illustrated by Lucy Fleming
    Summary: The classic fairy tale of Cinderella comes to life with music and full-color illustrations.
    ISBN: 978-1-63290-552-9 (library binding/CD)
    ISBN: 978-1-63290-568-0 (paperback/CD)
Suggested Dewey and Subject Headings:
    Dewey: E 398.2
    LCSH Subject Headings: Fairy tales – Juvenile literature. | Fairy tales – Songs and music – Texts. | Fairy tales – Juvenile sound recordings.
    Sears Subject Headings: Fairy tales. | Princesses. | School songbooks. | Children's songs. | Popular music.
    BISAC Subject Headings: JUVENILE FICTION / Fairy Tales & Folklore / Adaptations. | JUVENILE FICTION / Stories in Verse. | JUVENILE FICTION / Royalty.

Book design and art direction, Tim Palin Creative
Editorial direction, Flat Sole Studio
Music direction, Elizabeth Draper
Music arranged and produced by Drew Temperante

Printed in the United States of America in North Mankato, Minnesota.
072016   0335CGF16

ACCESS THE MUSIC!

SCAN CODE WITH MOBILE APP

CANTATALEARNING.COM

Children all over the world have heard the fairy tale about a girl named Ella. She worked hard cooking and cleaning for her **stepmother**. Because she slept near the fireplace, she was always covered with **cinders**. That's how she got the nickname Cinderella.

To find out if Cinderella lives happily ever after, turn the page and sing along!

Oh, Cinderella, once upon a dream,
lived with her stepmother, who was quite mean.

To the prince's **ball**, she wanted to go,
but her mean stepmom said, "No, no, no!"

Hey, Cinderella, so strong and bright, keep your chin up. You will win this fight.

Don't let the bad things bring you down. Someday soon you will wear a crown.

8

Her fairy **godmother**, all dressed in white,
helped Cinderella get to the ball that night—
a bit of magic right before her eyes,
and sparkly glass **slippers**, the perfect size.

She and the handsome prince danced toe to toe.
Then the clock struck twelve, and she had to go!

She ran from the ball. The prince ran after,
but all he found was her glass slipper.

13

Hey, Cinderella, so strong and bright,
keep your chin up. You will win this fight.

Don't let the bad things bring you down.
Someday soon you will wear a crown.

The prince went looking, slipper in hand.
Girls tried it on from across the land.

No foot was a perfect fit, it's true,
until Cinderella slipped on that shoe.

To the castle, the prince took her away,
and he married Cinderella that day.

The birds sang, and the halls filled with laughter.
They both lived happily ever after.

Hey, Cinderella, so strong and bright,
keep your chin up. You will win this fight.

Don't let the bad things bring you down.
Someday soon you will wear a crown.

SONG LYRICS
Cinderella

Oh, Cinderella, once upon a dream,
lived with her stepmother, who was quite mean.
To the prince's ball, she wanted to go,
but her mean stepmom said, "No, no, no!"

Hey, Cinderella, so strong and bright,
keep your chin up. You will win this fight.
Don't let the bad things bring you down.
Someday soon you will wear a crown.

Her fairy godmother, all dressed in white,
helped Cinderella get to the ball that night—
a bit of magic right before her eyes
and sparkly glass slippers, the perfect size.

She and the handsome prince danced toe to toe.
Then the clock struck twelve, and she had to go!
She ran from the ball. The prince ran after,
but all he found was her glass slipper.

Hey, Cinderella, so strong and bright,
keep your chin up. You will win this fight.
Don't let the bad things bring you down.
Someday soon you will wear a crown.

The prince went looking, slipper in hand.
Girls tried it on from across the land.
No foot was a perfect fit, it's true,
until Cinderella slipped on that shoe.

To the castle, the prince took her away,
and he married Cinderella that day.
The birds sang, and the halls filled with laughter.
They both lived happily ever after.

Hey, Cinderella, so strong and bright,
keep your chin up. You will win this fight.
Don't let the bad things bring you down.
Someday soon you will wear a crown.

Cinderella

Hip Hop
Drew Temperante

Verse

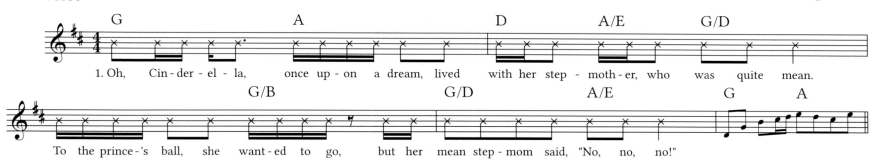

1. Oh, Cin - der - el - la, once up - on a dream, lived with her step - moth - er, who was quite mean.

To the prince -'s ball, she want - ed to go, but her mean step - mom said, "No, no, no!"

Chorus

Hey, Cin - der - el - la, so strong and bright, keep your chin up. You will win this fight. Don't let the

bad things bring you down. Some-day soon you will wear a crown.

Verse 2
Her fairy godmother, all dressed in white,
helped Cinderella get to the ball that night—
a bit of magic right before her eyes
and sparkly glass slippers, the perfect size.

Verse 3
She and the handsome prince danced toe to toe.
Then the clock struck twelve, and she had to go!
She ran from the ball. The prince ran after,
but all he found was her glass slipper.

Chorus

Verse 4
The prince went looking, slipper in hand.
Girls tried it on from across the land.
No foot was a perfect fit, it's true,
until Cinderella slipped on that shoe.

Verse 5
To the castle, the prince took her away,
and he married Cinderella that day.
The birds sang, and the halls filled with laughter.
They both lived happily ever after.

Chorus

GLOSSARY

ball—an elegant dance party

cinders—small pieces of wood or coal that have been partly burned

godmother—a woman who promises to support a child

slippers—slide-on shoes

stepmother—a woman who marries a person's father after the death or divorce of the person's mother

GUIDED READING ACTIVITIES

1. Cinderella lost a shoe as she rushed to get home. Have you ever lost something that was important to you? What was it, and why was it important?

2. If you had a fairy godmother, what one wish would you make, and why?

3. Cinderella gets married and lives in a castle. What do you think it would be like living in a castle? Draw a picture of a castle that you would like to live in.

TO LEARN MORE

Braun, Eric, Nancy Loewen, and Trisha Speed Shaskan. *The Other Side of the Story: Fairy Tales from a Different Perspective.* North Mankato, MN: Picture Window Books, a Capstone imprint, 2014.

Lagonegro, Melissa. *Cinderella.* New York: Random House, 2012.

Meister, Cari. *Cinderella: 4 Beloved Tales.* North Mankato, MN: Picture Window Books, a Capstone imprint, 2015.

Underwood, Deborah. *Interstellar Cinderella.* San Francisco: Chronicle Books, 2015.